Daddy Hairdo

FRANCIS MARTIN

CLAIRE POWELL

SIMON & SCHUSTER
London   New York   Sydney   Toronto   New Delhi

When Amy was born,
she didn't have much hair.

Dad, on the other hand,

had LOTS.

Then Amy and Dad had the
same amount of hair.

Then Amy had more hair than
Dad and Dad's hair just started . . .

disappearing.

Amy tried to help Dad look for it

but it had gone.

For good.

Amy and Dad looked in books.
Where does hair go when it goes?

Does it go off around the world . . .

in search of hair-raising adventures?

Or does it just disappear
down the plughole?

Dad's missing hair
was nowhere to be found.

But in the meantime,
Amy's hair grew . . .

and grew . . .

and GREW.

Just look at it all!

It took **a lot** of looking after.

On windy days,

it was a right nuisance.

When it got tangled,
the cat had to comb it.

On rainy days, it got so wet
Amy had to dry it on a washing line.

And when she played hide-and-seek,

Amy was **ALWAYS** found.

Soon, it was so long she couldn't even stand on the floor any more and had to be carried around.

In spite of all this, Amy **loved** her hair. She wasn't going to go to just any hairdresser.

DAD would have to think of something.

So he studied . . .

and he practised . . .

until finally he was
ready to reveal . . .

. . . the Daddy Hairdo!

Dad created . . .

'The Ice Cream Cone',

'The Rings of Saturn',

'The Castle in the Clouds'

and, his personal favourite,

'The Triple Beehive'.

Amy was a sensation!

And Dad's hairdos were
the talk of the town.

Everybody loved them.

But 'The Castle in the Clouds' made
hide-and-seek even MORE difficult . . .

there were some places that
'The Ice Cream Cone' wasn't allowed into . . .

. . . and, worst of all, 'The Triple Beehive' wouldn't fit through the doorway of Sweet Sensations.

Enough
was
enough.

So that's when Dad took Amy for her favourite Daddy Hairdo of all.

(And Amy **still** had more hair than Dad!)